AMKL.

£1.65

THOMAS
ONETWO

THOMAS ONETWO

by Ernest M. Robson

Illustrations by Ken Friedman

Something Else Press, Inc.
New York   1971

MANUFACTURED IN THE UNITED STATES OF AMERICA

ISBN 0-87110-074-6

Publisher's Foreword

Some people know Ernest M. Robson as one of the main popularizers of Astronomy, among semi-amateurs and semi-professionals. Others know him as one of the guys who flooded a street with suds in the course of inventing rug shampoo. True, he has been a chemist, at least professionally. And a trapper. And, presently, a lecturer on the structural and theoretical aspects of poetry, with his wife, who has done a great deal of the execution of the orthography of poetry which Robson proposed. Robson's older book, *The Orchestra of the Language* (Thomas Yoseloff, New York, 1959) was highly controversial in its implications. The Science department at *Saturday Review* dealt with it at length, and raised the wrath of no less than their own poetry editor, John Ciardi. Until Robson's findings were verified in 1969, the controversy continued. Robson's more recent book, *Transwhichics* (Dufour Publishing, Chester Springs, Pa. 1970), deals more specifically with the orthography and technology of using sound in literature. It details the Robson orthog-

raphy, which is of increasing interest for those involved in teaching the deaf to speak, and it exemplifies the kind of vowel cognate structures (common in such vowel-harmony languages as Turkish but rare in English) that provide the underpinnings for Robson's own poetry, a generous selection of which is included in the book.

Because, ultimately Robson is a scientist poet. The works cannot be divorced from their research element without causing real damage to them. Robson researches not structure but the form of his own subjects. In this sense he up-ends other scientist poets such as Buckminster Fuller. He is in the best sense a rhetorician, concerned less with how to say something effectively than with the whole dynamic of saying it at all.

Thomas Onetwo bears a relation to Ernest Robson's works similar to that of *Alice's Adventures Underground* — or perhaps, better, *The Hunting of the Snark* — to Lewis Carroll's. Everybody knows Carroll was a *nom de plume* for a celebrated Victorian mathematician. There's the famous story that Queen Victoria, having enjoyed *Alice,* asked her chancellor to buy for her the complete works of that "marvelous writer whom *we* so enjoy"— and was *she* ever surprised: But *Thomas Onetwo* is *very* prophetic. It anticipates the attitudes of pop art— perhaps of Robson's own involvement with rug shampoo, for instance. And the world it described in 1926 is frighteningly identical with the world of 1971, 45 years later. The whole intervening liberal epoch did not, apparently, change the country or its regions much. And the various protests that are happening today seem appropriate to the world of Thomas O'Nettwoe (as we call him) although they don't happen explicitly.

Those who think are often relevant outside their so-called field of competence. Occasionally they are also delightful. And it's in this spirit that we are presenting (some 45 years late) Ernest M. Robson's prose fantasy, *Thomas One-two*.

The Publishers
February, 1971

Author's Preface

Thomas Onetwo, written in 1926, an experiment in fiction, attempted to solve the problem of summarizing a variety of ideas and emotions around the distribution of a commodity. This it achieved. In view of contemporary Pop Art and the many similarities between the Roaring Twenties and the Mad Sixties this picaresque refrain on a pickle may suggest its parallels.

There are philosophic implications in this booklet. It has been one of the few (possibly only) attempts to cast advertising in the form of serious literature. The seriousness was as naive as the story in its rejection of hucksterism in favor of consumption as a blessed event and a palliative for the tragedy of existence. But ... will this viewpoint *always* be considered naive?

THOMAS
ONETWO

i

Thomas Onetwo left Missouri to become President of the United States. On the road he met a young man with whom he became friendly. When he awoke next morning, all the cash he had saved in Missouri was gone.

He asked his friend, "Did you find any money?"

"No," said the tramp.

"I believe you," said Thomas.

Now,

if that man Thomas Onetwo had eaten a jar of Mrs. Baker's pickles, before he met that tramp on the road, it looks very much as if he would have been robbed just the same,

But,

and here's the point,

he would have had a few more pleasant moments, Because of the delicious flavor in Mrs. Baker's pickles.

After being robbed of all the money he had saved in Missouri, Thomas Onetwo got a job in a garage.

One afternoon, he looked up from his well-thumbed outline, "How to become President of the United States," to hear a friend of his say,

"People only have two wisdom teeth."

"They don't either," said a mechanic, "They have four."

"You're a fool," replied the other.

"Let's settle it," said the mechanic, doubling up his fists.

"All right," said Onetwo's friend, and he was promptly knocked out by a punch on the jaw.

Thomas Onetwo

Now,

    if that friend of Thomas One-
two's had eaten a jar of Mrs. Baker's
pickles, it is more than likely that people
would have four wisdom teeth just the
same, and that he would nevertheless
have been knocked out by a punch on
the jaw,

    But,

       and here's the point,

            he would
have had a few more pleasant moments,
Because of the delicious flavor in Mrs.
Baker's pickles.

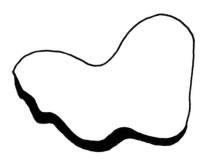

iii

Why aren't you working?" asked the boss at the garage.

"I'm reading 'How to become President of the United States'," answered Thomas Onetwo.

The boss lost his temper and said, "You're a damn fool."

Thomas thought for hours and hours how he could pay back that insult. Three days later he walked over to the boss's house and said,

"So are you," and was fired.

Thomas Onetwo

Now,

if that man Thomas Onetwo
had eaten a jar of Mrs. Baker's pickles,
the chances are he would have made
that more or less brilliant comeback just
the same, and his services would no
longer have been craved at that garage,

But,

and here's the point,

he would
have had a few more pleasant moments,
Because of the delicious flavor in Mrs.
Baker's pickles.

iv

Do you know that the pope is going to be President of the United States?" said a gentleman to Thomas Onetwo in a gent's room in the area of the Chicagoans.

"No," replied T. Onetwo, "I'm going to become President of the U.S.A."

"Where the hell did you come from to doubt my word?" inquired the gentleman.

"I'm from Missouri," answered Thomas.

"I'll bet you're a Catholic, and nobody can call me a liar, especially about the pope," roared the gentleman, and he scooped up and threw a handful of liquid soap in Thomas's eyes and ran out of the gentlemen's room.

Thomas Onetwo

Now,

if Thomas Onetwo had eaten
a jar of Mrs. Baker's pickles, he still
would have been abused in that gentlemen's room in the area of the Chicagoans for having doubted that the pope
was trying to become President of the
United States,

But,

and here's the point,

he would
have had a few more pleasant moments,
Because of the delicious flavor in Mrs.
Baker's pickles.

Thomas Onetwo applied to the Mendax Insurance Company for a salesman's job.

Mr. Mendax said to him, "Young man, do you realize we are all salesmen? Salesmanship is the vital force not only in business but in morality and good citizenship. The parent sells the child the value of right living; the school teacher must sell the child the facts that are in the text book; and so on through all life. One of our tasks in this organization, and one of our opportunities, is to sell the spirit of progress."

"How much do you charge people for it?" asked Thomas Onetwo, and he didn't get the job.

Now,

      if Thomas Onetwo had eaten a jar of Mrs. Baker's pickles, there isn't much doubt that he would still have asked that foolish question which made Mr. Mendax refuse him the job,

But,

      and here's the point,

                he would have had a few more pleasant moments, Because of the delicious flavor in Mrs. Baker's pickles.

$\mathbb{A}$t the employment agency, Thomas Onetwo met a minister who asked him what he was going to do.

"I'm trying to become President of the United States," answered Thomas.

"And why do you want to be President?"

"So I can make everybody happy," said Thomas.

"But do you know what makes everybody unhappy?" asked the minister.

"The source of all the sorrows of the people in the United States is that they have no religion. In the uncolored perfume of old songs, we were born divine, but now the spirit of God broods no more upon the waters; money is really the only thing that holds this people together, and no nation can live long on such a principle."

And he sighed.

Thomas Onetwo

Now,

if that minister had eaten a
jar of Mrs. Baker's pickles, he would
have been forced to go to an employment agency just the same, and he
would have been just as deeply grieved
over the decay of religion,

But,

and here's the point,

he would
have had a few more pleasant moments,
Because of the delicious flavor in Mrs.
Baker's pickles.

Thomas Onetwo rented a room from a professor of Greek at Slickwick University, and said to him one evening as they were walking past a row of fraternity houses,

"A minister told me the source of all the sorrows of the people in the United States is that they have no religion."

"That may well be," said the professor, "but I should presume to say, it is because the school curricula do not emphasize the classics nearly enough, therefore the people do not read Greek, and so nobody realizes what only Plato knew,—that simplicity and truth and beauty are one, and that only from these can goodness arise."

Just then one of the initiates leaned out the window of a fraternity house and hit the professor in the neck with a rotten tomato.

"Ai, Ai, Hyacynthus," cried the professor, and walked on.

Thomas Onetwo

Now,

if that professor of Greek had
eaten a jar of Mrs. Baker's pickles, he
probably would still have thought that
ignorance of Greek was the cause of all
the sorrows of America, and would have
been hit in the neck with a rotten tomato just the same,

But,

and here's the point,

he would
have had a few more pleasant moments,
Because of the delicious flavor in Mrs.
Baker's pickles.

viii

Mr. A. B. Louse leaned out of the tower of the A.B.C.D. Louse & Company building, and gazing over the city of the Chicagoans, addressed his employees: "The glory that was Greece, and the grandeur that was Rome,—Yes, a pretty good old line in its day, I'll quote you a better one,—Santa Claus this year is going to give us a $342,000,000 Christmas present,—total building volume for Chicago 1925. Laugh that off, Greece and Rome. Oh, hum."

"But, Mr. Louse," interrupted Thomas Onetwo, in spite of the crowd, "back in Missouri, Professor Oyster used to say that some Roman homes had plumbing and were as good as we've got today."

And in spite of the crowd, Mr. A. B. Louse cried,

"Whoever said that is dismissed."

Thomas Onetwo

Now,

even if that man Thomas Onetwo had eaten a jar of Mrs. Baker's pickles, he probably would have uttered that same innocent and inopportune remark which infuriated Mr. Louse to the point of dismissing him,

But,

and here's the point,

Thomas would have had a few more pleasant moments, Because of the delicious flavor in Mrs. Baker's pickles.

I'm going to the Flea Circus," said Thomas Onetwo. "I've been kicked out of enough jobs. I guess I need education."

When he got to the circus, he saw a Flea Scientist standing by a table on which were strolling many fleas in white coats and black hats. The Scientist rang a bell and all the fleas jerked their knees. Then he took a bunny out of his pocket and all the fleas began to tremble.

"I will now show you Willie," said the Scientist, "Whom I made into a genius by keeping him tied to a wheelbarrow for seven weeks. Come here, Willie."

The flea sat down on a piano stool.

xi

Thomas Onetwo became a footman on a Rolls Royce belonging to the swellest lady in West Indiana and one afternoon while holding the door open for her to get out, he asked,

"Madam, you have been looking so worried lately, could you tell me the source of all sorrows?"

"Yes, Thomas," answered his mistress. "It's because my dog is homosexual."

"I don't understand that," answered Thomas.

"I didn't either," replied the lady, "until I took Sardonapolis to the most expensive interpreter of dog dreams in West Indiana. Dr. Bill first gave him an intelligence test and found that he remembered certain things very well.

Then he fed him a pound of raw sirloin steak, and after that made him recline on a rug near a stove. As soon as Sardonapolis fell asleep, the doctor clapped a seismographic sort of apparatus to his member and stealthily introduced into the room a white bitch sealed up in a celluloid box which he placed near Sardonapolis's nose. Sardonapolis reacted immediately by softly growling and rolling over, which disrupted the apparatus but not soon enough to spoil the record of the dream. The doctor said he was affected with megalocanino-pseudovenalogica which is serious though not as dangerous as hydrophobia and strongly recommended his playing with fur bags and old slippers, and I don't see why that shouldn't have been the right cure because Dr. Bill is publishing an "Outline of Dog Psychology."

"This morning Providence seemed to influence a yellow bitch with red eyes to approach Sardonapolis on our front lawn, and even though her pedigree was questionable, I prayed,—but what do you suppose Sardonapolis did? He turned his back on her and started licking our hydrant; and *now* what shall I do?"

Thomas Onetwo

Now,

if that swell Society lady of West Indiana had eaten a jar of Mrs. Baker's pickles, she would have been just as worried because her dog Sardonapolis was afflicted with megalocaninopseudo-venalogica,

But,

and here's the point,

she would have had a few more moments of plea-sure, Because of the delicious flavor in Mrs. Baker's pickles.

homas Onetwo became the butler of a blond lady who lived in the land of the Terre Haughtians and who was ardently wooed by a professional clown and a professional critic. The three of them sat in such a gloom one night that Thomas said,

"Pardon me, madam and gentlemen, but can you tell me the source of all sorrows of the American people?"

The professional clown answered, "It's humor. Humor is that cowardice which allows no man to speak what he really feels, even to his love."

The critic answered, "You clowns who must have secret tears in your soul bore me. As if everybody didn't have them. Your humor is a real form because the logic of negation and distortion hold some truth. But consider the critic. Art works which are the stuff of his living have no real approach to a comprehensive audience, because they

— 24 —

haven't as yet discovered a clear-speaking vehicle which can communicate with that audience in a biologically essential way, and through which alone people can come to feel the importance of their lives as a part of this whole civilization. *On account* of this unreal quality of his own material the critic's world becomes relatively unimportant, because, only in the destruction of these art forms can *his* work achieve form. Can anything be more pitiful?"

The blond lady said, "Thomas, bring in a jar of Mrs. Baker's pickles."

xiii

Thomas Onetwo met a young girl sitting on a curbstone and sighing in the suburbs of the Indianapoleons. He addressed her,

"How do you do, Miss Indianapoleon, won't you tell me the source of all the sorrows of the American people?"

"I was class valedictorian at Utopia High," she said. "The biggest high school in the country of the Indianapoleons, and I graduated with flying honors. The teachers and textbooks all impressed me with the wonders of this country and what an important place I was to fill in it, and then when I got out into the world, I discovered I was almost nothing in a great big steel system. I think the source of all the sorrows of the American people is that when they are young they are taught to expect much too much from life."

Thomas Onetwo

Now,

      if that valedictorian of Utopia High had eaten a jar of Mrs. Baker's pickles, the odds still hold that she would have been just as bitterly disillusioned when she really began to experience this civilization for herself and understand her place in it,

    But,

      and here's the point,

            she would have experienced a few more pleasant moments, Because of the delicious flavor in Mrs. Baker's pickles.

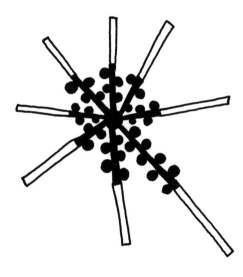

xiv

Thomas Onetwo came to the banks of the Wabash and roomed next to an optimist whom he asked about the source of all the sorrows in America.

"There are none to speak of," smiled the optimist, and chanted:
"We are the children of the
rising sun,
The moving of rainbows
And bright music
Through prisms in the sky."

"Then why were you so sad and sighing so much last night when I passed your room?" asked T. Onetwo.

"I was depressed that everybody in the world wasn't as happy as I am," replied the optimist.

Thomas Onetwo

Now,

   if that optimist had eaten a
jar of Mrs. Baker's pickles, he still would
have had those few melancholy moments, because everybody wasn't as happy as he was,

   But,

      and here's the point,

         even
though he was an optimist he would
have had even more pleasant moments,
Because of the delicious flavor in Mrs.
Baker's pickles.

XV

The most pessimistic and intellectual street cleaner in Kankakee stood next to a manhole smirking in the country of the Kankakeeans.

"What is the source of all sorrows in America," asked Thomas Onetwo.

"The beginning of things," groaned the street cleaner. "Our griefs are greater than our pleasures. We are born in pain and die in pain. The only thing to do is suicide."

"Lookout," shouted Thomas Onetwo, as he saw a limousine tearing towards them.

And the intellectual street cleaner jumped safely into the manhole.

Thomas Onetwo

Now,
        if that pessimistic street clean-
er had eaten a jar of Mrs. Baker's pickles,
he still would have had the great mis-
fortune not to have been run over and
killed by that limousine,
    But,
        and here's the point,
                he would
have had a few more pleasant moments,
Because of the delicious flavor in Mrs.
Baker's pickles.

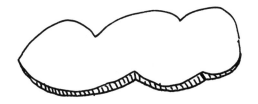

Thomas Onetwo sat next to a lady at a cafeteria who scowled so hard that he asked her what was the source of all the sorrows of the American people.

"Brokers and middle-men," she said, "are the source of all our sorrows. They feed on large scale industry which makes people slave at hateful routine tasks that crush the spirit out of them."

"But," asked T. Onetwo, "what do you mean by brokers and middle-men?"

"They are the men who produce less and get more pay than anybody else in the world."

"Then that solves everything," said Thomas. "There's only one thing to do, and that's to kill all the brokers and middle-men in America."

"I'm not so sure about that," replied the lady, "but this I do know,— they have so outrageously robbed the people, that the time will come, and no one hates to see it more than I, when there will be revolution," and here a look of sadness passed over her face.

Thomas Onetwo

Now,

if that radical lady had eaten
a jar of Mrs. Baker's pickles, that look
of sadness would have passed over her
face just the same, because of that in-
evitable revolution against the brokers
and middle-men,

But,

and here's the point,

she would
have had a few more pleasant moments,
Because of the delicious flavor in Mrs.
Baker's pickles.

Will killing all the brokers and middle-men remove the source of all the sorrows in the United States?" Thomas Onetwo asked the famous philosopher Do-We, who was standing on a street car track thinking in the city of the Southbendians.

"There are three reasons against such a procedure," answered the philosopher.

"1.—they are at present a necessary part of our economic order,

2.—there are too many of them,

3.—such a methodology is inexpedient, or, shall I say, unpragmatic. But,"—and here he became so absorbed that he didn't see a street car heading towards him, "the origin of our sorrows lies in the event that though Time is beyond us, it is absolutely necessary for us to live in Time-Space, in a limited Universe where Space is what we see," —when the street car interrupted him by running over his toe.

Thomas Onetwo

Now,

if that famous philosopher had eaten a jar of Mrs. Baker's pickles, he still would have been fated to live in Time-Space, and would have got his toe run over by a Southbendian street car just the same,

But,

and here's the point,

he would have had a few more pleasant moments, Because of the delicious flavor in Mrs. Baker's pickles.

Thomas Onetwo came upon a young woman sitting by the roadside alone, and weeping.

"What's the matter, Miss?" asked Thomas Onetwo.

"Leave me alone," she said.

"But I'm looking for the source of all the sorrows of the American people, so won't you tell me what you are crying for?"

"I was a nice June bride," she said, "and my husband left me."

"But I don't see why," said Thomas.

"Neither do I," the young woman went on, "He said he was looking for a Chinese woman, I couldn't sing in the morning, he missed his pool game, he couldn't sleep and, besides, he had halitosis," and she got up and walked away.

Thomas Onetwo

Now,

if that ex-June bride had served her husband a jar of Mrs. Baker's pickles, it is much more than likely that her husband would have left her just the same,

But,

and here's the point,

they would have enjoyed at least a few moments of pleasure together, Because of the delicious taste of Mrs. Baker's pickles.

xix

Thomas Onetwo went to the country of the Ohioeons and sat next to a clergyman on a park bench whom he asked about the source of all the sorrows of the people in the United States.

The clergyman replied, "The source of all America's sorrows is liquor," and pulling an aluminum bible from his pocket, he took a long swig of Scotch.

"Then why do you drink?" asked Thomas.

"No one understood the saints," sighed the clergyman, "I drink to save mankind from as much liquor as possible." And two tears rolled down his cheeks.

Thomas Onetwo

Now,

if that clergyman had eaten
a jar of Mrs. Baker's pickles, he would
have been drinking just as much Scotch
for the sake of mankind, and would
have been misunderstood just the same,

But,

and here's the point,

he would

have had a few compensatory moments,
Because of the delicious flavor in Mrs.
Baker's pickles.

Thomas Onetwo became janitor for two wealthy women in the country of the Pittsburghians.

"Now ladies, what *IS* the source of all the sorrows of the people of America?" asked T. Onetwo.

"Ambition, Thomas," one of the ladies replied, "is the source of the people's sorrow. It's ambition that makes men live only in the future and lose all the pleasure of little things in the present. It kills love and perverts all forms of life."

The other lady said, "I don't give a snap about the people. My sorrow is that I was born a woman. I know that so-called liberated women have been efficient in many ways, but only men can do real things. Every month I realize again my destiny is wasted unless I bear children, and even that compensation is a pain and a sorrow."

The first lady said, "You've proved my point."

Thomas Onetwo

Now,

      if those two wealthy Pittsburghian ladies had each eaten a jar of Mrs. Baker's pickles, they would have been just as sad over destiny,

    But,

       and here's the point,

                they would have had a few more pleasant moments, Because of the delicious flavor in Mrs. Baker's pickles.

Thomas Onetwo became acquainted with an up-to-date poet in the country of the Catskillians whom he asked,

"You seem so glum, I wonder if you know the source of all the sorrows of the American people?"

"Yes," said the poet, and recited:
"The substitution of words for
nitrogen breeds perfume
"undulating through walls of
bones,
"and rolling man's muscles in
long billows over the land.
"It ties up the earth with iron,
"and procreating sobs for time-
less butterflies,
"makes pink perfumed mice
"for pets."

"Well, what's that got to do with the source of all sorrows?" interrupted T. Onetwo.

Thomas Onetwo

The poet groaned, "You don't understand," to which Thomas replied, "I don't see anything in that to understand." Whereupon the modern poet lost control of himself and started to pelt Thomas with his unpublished works. Thomas promptly took out of his pocket his well-thumbed little outline "How to become President of the United States" and slapped the poet in the face with it.

Now,

if Thomas Onetwo and that poet had eaten a jar of Mrs. Baker's pickles together, it is highly improbable that they would have understood each other any better,

But,

and here's the point,

they could have had a few more pleasant moments in each other's company, Because of the delicious flavor in Mrs. Baker's pickles.

xxii

Two Jews were the first people Thomas Onetwo met in New York City. He walked down Broadway with them and asked whether they knew the source of all the sorrows of the American people.

One Jew said, "I can't answer for all the people in the United States, but, for me, the bitterest grief I know is that I was ever born a Jew."

The second Jew replied, "Why do you talk about the Jews in such a way? Don't you know the Jews are the greatest people in the world?"

To which the first Jew answered, "The Jews control everything in New York but themselves."

Whereupon, to Thomas's astonishment, the other Jew blurted out, "You dirty kike," and walked away.

Thomas Onetwo

Now,

if those two Jews had eaten a
jar of Mrs. Baker's pickles, they nevertheless would have realized the sorrow
that they were Jews,

But,

and here's the point,

they both
would have had a few more pleasant
moments, Because of the delicious flavor
in Mrs. Baker's pickles.

Thomas Onetwo walked by a building on a hill, searching for the source of all the sorrows in America. Suddenly, a voice from behind a window shouted, "The sorrow at the center of the Universe is mathematics,—one, two, one, two, one, two,—hi there!"

Thomas rushed into the building and said to a man dressed in white, "Somebody is calling me."

"What makes you think so?" asked the doctor, "What did they say?"

"Onetwo, Onetwo," answered Thomas.

"Dementia praecox," muttered the doctor to a nurse as Thomas was hurried away to the ward for the violently insane.

Thomas Onetwo

Now,

      if that man Thomas Onetwo
had eaten a jar of Mrs. Baker's pickles,
he still would have been not unpain-
fully relegated to the violent ward in the
hospital for the insane under the label
"Dementia praecox,"

But,

      and here's the point,

            he would
have had a few more pleasant moments,
Because of the delicious flavor in Mrs.
Baker's pickles.

xx*iv*

"**S**ex is the source of all our sorrows," said a man standing on the lawn in front of the hospital for the insane.

"Then why do you keep looking at the sky all day long through that magnifying glass?" asked Thomas Onetwo.

"I'm trying to find out how much of the wish to be loved lies in the Sun," answered the man.

Thomas Onetwo

Now,

if that insane man had eaten
a jar of Mrs. Baker's pickles, he still
would have been trying to find out how
much of the wish to be loved lies in the
sun,

But,

and here's the point,

he would
have had a few more pleasant moments,
Because of the delicious flavor in Mrs.
Baker's pickles.

XXV

In the hospital for the insane was a clinic to which Thomas Onetwo was invited. He stood in front of a group of people who gazed intently at him while the doctor patted him on the back and said,

"Thomas is a very likeable fellow, he's searching for the cause of all the sorrows in America, something we'd all like to know, wouldn't we, Thomas?"

"Yes, Doctor," answered Thomas.

"Thomas and I are really good friends," then turning to his audience, the doctor said, "Tell us, Thomas, what you've been doing for your sex life."

"Yes, Doctor," answered Thomas.

The doctor whispered something in Thomas's ear and he replied: "I don't know what you fellows did, but, I, masturbated."

Thomas Onetwo

Now,

      if that man Thomas Onetwo
had eaten a jar of Mrs. Baker's pickles,
that is still what he would probably
have done for his sex life,

    But,

      and here's the point,

                he would
have had a few more pleasant moments,
Because of the delicious flavor in Mrs.
Baker's pickles.

In the hospital for the insane, Thomas Onetwo came upon a man holding a moist sponge out of the window, and asked him what he was doing.

"With this sponge full of tears, I measure how rapidly the earth draws the great western winds under the sun," replied the man.

"Say, any guy as sad as you ought to know the source of all the sorrows in America," said T. Onetwo.

"Science is the source of all sorrows," answered the man. "When I was young and believed in myself, I thought man needed only to discover scientific laws in order to govern nature, but then I learned man's emotions were also part of nature, and like all other things are enslaved by these laws. We are machines, and all is futile," and he put the sponge up to his eyes and leaned out of the window again.

Thomas Onetwo

Now,

if that man in the hospital for the insane, had eaten a jar of Mrs. Baker's pickles, it is quite likely he would still have been trying to find out how rapidly the earth draws the great western winds under the sun,

But,

and here's the point,

he would have had a few more pleasant moments, Because of the delicious flavor in Mrs. Baker's pickles.

xxvii

In the insane asylum one of Thomas Onetwo's friends said, "I'm Christ."

A neighboring friend announced, "That's a lie. *I'm Christ.*"

When they continued arguing even more angrily, Thomas interrupted them saying, "Please, fellows, be reasonable. After all, neither of you is Christ."

"Let the devils be cast out of ye! Be gone!" roared the second Christ, and while T. Onetwo was stumbling over a chair to escape and spraining his ankle, the other Christ held up his hand pleading,

"Brothers, be gentle, the foxes have their lairs and the birds in the sky their nests, but where has the Son of Man to lay his head?"

Thomas Onetwo

Now,

          if that man Thomas Onetwo
had eaten a jar of Mrs. Baker's pickles,
he nevertheless would have suffered in
the insane asylum from a sprained
ankle,

      But,

          and here's the point,

                    he would
have had a few more pleasant moments,
Because of the delicious flavor in Mrs.
Baker's pickles.

Y ou need a lady who will be perfectly friendly with you," said the doctor as he dismissed Thomas Onetwo from the hospital for the insane.

On the way out, Thomas stopped a policemen whom he asked,

"I'm touring America to find the most perfect lady in the world. Where do you think I ought to begin?" and the policeman took him right back to the hospital.

Now,

if Thomas Onetwo had eaten a jar of Mrs. Baker's pickles, he would still have thought that that policeman could tell him where to find the most perfect lady in the world and would have been promptly taken back to the hospital for the insane,

But,

and here's the point,

he would have had a few more pleasant moments, Because of the delicious flavor in Mrs. Baker's pickles.

Thomas Onetwo entered the country of the Trojans, New York, where he fell in love with a widow who told him he shouldn't bother her again until he was rich. So Thomas went into the bootlegging profession, and inside of three months, made enough money to feel sure of winning her.

When he returned to her apartment and discovered she had gone off with a big oil man, he became so dazed that he recklessly drove his liquor-laden car into a telephone pole, and was sent to jail for violating the eighteenth amendment!

Now,

if that man Thomas Onetwo had eaten a jar of Mrs. Baker's pickles, he still would have been sent to jail for bootlegging for that widow,
But,
and here's the point,
he would have had a few more pleasant moments, Because of the delicious flavor in Mrs. Baker's pickles.

In jail, Thomas Onetwo's cell-mate asked him,

"What are you going to do when you get out?"

"I'm going to keep on touring America to find the most perfect lady in the world. What are you going to do?"

"I'm going to do four more years for not supporting a wife," answered the man, and after that he hardly ever spoke to Thomas.

Now,

if that man Thomas Onetwo had eaten a jar of Mrs. Baker's pickles, he nevertheless would have made his prison term even more unpleasant by antagonizing his cellmate,

But,

and here's the point,

he would have had a few more pleasant moments, Because of the delicious flavor in Mrs. Baker's pickles.

xxxi

Freed from jail, Thomas One-two wanted to find the most perfect lady in America so badly that he became friendly with a social worker in New York City and asked her what he should do.

"Why don't you go into social service work?" she suggested. "That will give you something worthwhile to do for society which will help make the world safe for the perfect lady to be born into and brought up in, if, as you say you haven't already succeeded in finding her."

"What? You say she isn't born yet? I don't care what you mean by society, I want my perfect lady now."

And they separated.

Thomas Onetwo

Now,
　　　　if Thomas Onetwo had eaten
a jar of Mrs. Baker's pickles, it appears
very probable he would have been just
as annoyed by that social worker,
　　But,
　　　　and here's the point,
　　　　　　　　he would
have had a few more pleasant moments,
Because of the delicious flavor in Mrs.
Baker's pickles.

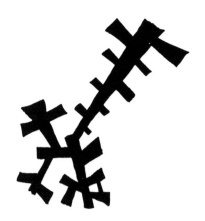

T here are all kinds of perfect ladies in Greenwich Village," said a taxi driver, so Thomas Onetwo went to the Wistful Lilly Tea Room, and sat behind a creature whose beauty attracted him with such intensity that he left his seat and introduced himself, saying:

"I have been looking all over America for the most perfect lady in the world, and you certainly . . .". . . when to his horror, he discovered the creature was a man who further horrified him by tapping his spoon against a glass and by crying, "Tinkle, tinkle, clattah, clattah, crash, crash,—such an adorable idea!" And a titter vibrated through the Wistful Lily.

Thomas Onetwo

Now,

if the man Thomas Onetwo
had eaten a jar of Mrs. Baker's pickles,
he would have been just as stunned and
would have made just as much of an ass
of himself at that Greenwich Village
tea room,

But,

and here's the point,

he would
have had a few more pleasant moments,
Because of the delicious flavor in Mrs.
Baker's pickles.

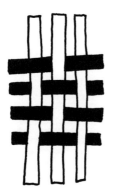

xxxiii

Thomas Onetwo went to a eugenicist and asked him,

"Where can I find the most perfect lady in the world?"

"Any where," answered the doctor, "as soon as her great-grandparents are immune on sixteen sides from hypersyphilosculabidinorumperomoritis.

"What does that mean, and how soon will it happen?" asked T. Onetwo.

"It means that this will take place when we can make people control themselves for sixteen generations," answered the eugenicist, and Thomas Onetwo, very much disappointed, went on his way.

Thomas Onetwo

Now,

   if that man T. Onetwo had
eaten a jar of Mrs. Baker's pickles, he
would have been just as dissatisfied and
disappointed by that word the doctor of
eugenics used,

   But,

      and here's the point,

         he would
have had a few more pleasant moments,
Because of the delicious flavor in Mrs.
Baker's pickles.

T homas Onetwo went to the western end of the land and asked a female artist with a white face and purple lips and green eyes if he could find the most perfect lady in the world at the Art Colony.

"No," she answered, "but I'll show you a picture of her I painted which is without any doubt the most perfect picture in the world."

Then she brought out a canvas decorated with a bright yellow rectangle slanted against a dark perpendicular line. On the upper part of the rectangle were two white circles. Above the white circles was a scarlet triangle.

"What do you think of her?" asked the artist.

"Of what?" asked Thomas.

"Why, your perfect lady, leaning against a pine tree, holding a poppy to her nose; and don't you care for the little green fish in her right hand?" indignantly asked the artist.

"Cut your kidding," guffawed Thomas.

Whereupon the artist said, "You are

very vulgar," and severed all relations with him.

Now,

    if that female artist had eaten a jar of Mrs. Baker's pickles, she would probably have been just as hurt by T. Onetwo's failure to appreciate her abstract painting,

But,

    and here's the point,

        she would have had a few more pleasant moments, Because of the delicious flavor in Mrs. Baker's pickles.

XXXV

Thomas Onetwo was invited to a midnight revel at the Art Colony because he knew of a painter in Missouri. All the artists got drunk and embraced each other saying,

"I like you."

"I don't like you."

A little man leaped on a table and standing above the crowd hollered out: "Demolishing reason,

let us revel in
with things like wings and fins
over rows of tiny houses
built from butter thins,
where little peanut-butter girls
wear onion petals in their curls
and chocolate puppy dogs
piss gallon cans of mayonnaise,
while evening clouds are colored
with a dash of chili sauce
to flavor off the sky
for a better day
descending on a desert island
in dark harbor bay,
where no white butterfly
or sailboat
floats away."

The little man then threw an alarm clock out the window, and the others began to hurl chairs and fling beer bottles until the question dawned on Thomas,

"Am I back in the insane asylum or not?" and in a great panic he rushed out into the night and fled from the Art Colony.

Now,

if that man Thomas Onetwo had eaten a jar of Mrs. Baker's pickles,

that midnight orgy at the Art Colony would have reminded him just as painfully of his visit in the hospital for the insane, and would have seared him just as much,

But,

and here's the point,

he would have had a few more pleasant moments, Because of the delicious flavor in Mrs. Baker's pickles.

xxxvi

As Thomas Onetwo was walking away from the Art Colony, he met a child sitting on a hedge and singing.

"What are you singing about, little girl?" asked Thomas.

"Day," she answered.

"Day?" repeated Onetwo.

"Yes, don't you know about day?" And she sang:

> *"Sweet is the morning dew*
> *"that sparkles on the string.*
> *"Sweet are the western winds*
> *"that over the mountains bring.*

> *"Sweet is the early morning beam,*
> *"the fast coming of day,*
> *"that passes through that lovely stream*
> *"in silence every day."*

"That's great," said Thomas, "I bet you grow up to be a big opera singer someday."

"No I won't either," she said. "When I grow up I'm going to be an ash man 'cause they have purple eyes."

Then the bell rang.

"I got to go to school but I hate to," she said as she ran off down the road.

Thomas Onetwo

Now,

      if that child had eaten a jar
of Mrs. Baker's pickles she would have
had to go to school the same as all the
other children,

But,

    and here's the point,

             she would
have had a few more pleasant moments,
Because of the delicious flavor in Mrs.
Baker's pickles.

xxxvii

Thomas Onetwo met a stranger coming out of the East in great haste whom he stopped and asked,

"Where's the best place in the land of the New Englanders to find the most perfect lady in the world?"

"Do you see this black eye?" replied the stranger, "this cut in my arm, and my torn clothes? That's what the good citizens of Rockling, New Hampshire gave me for talking about psychoanalysis. You *may* find your perfect lady in New England, though I doubt it, but let me assure you *this*, young man, Rockling, New Hampshire, is no place for a Freudian," and with even greater speed, he resumed his journey toward the city of the New Yorkers.

Thomas Onetwo

Now,

if that Freudian had eaten a
jar of Mrs. Baker's pickles, he still would
have been beaten up by those good
citizens of Rockling, New Hampshire,
But,

and here's the point,

he would
have had a few more pleasant moments,
Because of the delicious flavor in Mrs.
Baker's pickles.

xxxviii

After Thomas Onetwo had been in the land of the New Englanders a little while in search of the most perfect lady in the world, he ran so short of money that he was driven to beg for his food at farm houses.

Finally, a most Christian young woman took pity on him and gave him a plate of potatoes for sawing a cord of wood. Thomas became momentarily so flustered by her buxom figure that when he noticed there was no fork for him to eat his potatoes with, he said, "Madam, shall I go get a stork?"

Her husband, who had been concealed behind the door, rushed out and accused Thomas of lechery and adulterous designs. A town meeting was called and the selectmen sent Thomas such a violent threat that he fled from the land of the New Englanders forever.

Now,

if that man T. Onetwo had
eaten a jar of Mrs. Baker's pickles, he
probably would still have made that
most unfortunate slip, and would have
been forced to flee from the land of the
New Englanders in just as great a fear,

But,

and here's the point,

he would
have had a few more pleasant moments,
Because of the delicious flavor in Mrs.
Baker's pickles.

xxxix

Thomas Onetwo was walking toward the West when he met two prophets on the road whom he asked,

"Where can I find the most perfect lady in the world?"

The white prophet answered, "More general and efficient communication will level all walls, and make society One. A simpler language will arise, and there will be one capitol of the world in which senators from every land will sit. In spite of the apostles

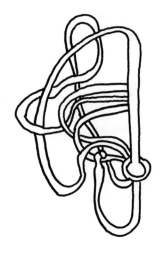

of Change, I know man would be happier in a Static order where he knew what he had to do without the pain of confusion. When the perfect man can stand on a hill and see the white city shine before his eyes, he will be able to die gracefully, and not until then will you find the perfect lady."

The copper colored prophet said, "You occidentals will never have peace and be at one with the universe until you accept death emotionally as well as theoretically. Are you not lonesome for the calm and wisdom of the East and do you not know that your world society is a quantitative thing that denies the quality of life and that its complexity removes it just so much further from true being?"

The white prophet replied, "I know complexity is such a sorrow, so beautiful, tomorrow thinning with disintegrating goverments; but, oh stranger, in the belly of each woman there wobbles a planet. I see dawn sparks floating in the night."

As soon as Thomas Onetwo heard the perfect lady couldn't be realized

now, he hurried away toward the West,
leaving the prophets standing alone.

    Now,
          if Thomas had eaten a jar of
Mrs. Baker's pickles, he still would
have been impatient to go on toward
the West in search of the perfect lady,
    But,
        and here's the point,
                    he would
have had a few more pleasant moments,
Because of the delicious flavor in Mrs.
Baker's pickles.

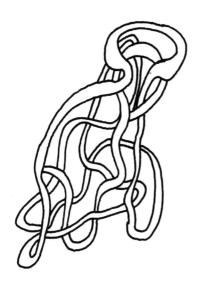

Thomas Onetwo went on toward the West into the country of the golden mountains where he fell in love with a French girl who manicured fingernails in the land of the Coloradolians. He told her,

"I've looked all over America for the most perfect lady in the world and you are she."

"No," replied Miss Brasblanc, "your perfect lady, and perhaps all perfect ladies, live too much in your mad seeking. If you would only stay in some one place and relax for a while and compose yourself you might find your perfect lady when you least expect her. Perhaps in the spring she will come down from the mountains. I am so sorry, Mr. Onetwo, but for now I can be nothing but a friend to you."

Thomas disregarded her advice, and wooed her so importunately that she left the country of the golden mountains. After she was gone he was so blinded with grief that he bumped into the Coloradolians on the streets.

Thomas Onetwo

Now,

if that man Thomas Onetwo
had eaten a jar of Mrs. Baker's pickles,
he nevertheless would have lost the
esteem of Miss Brasblanc, and would
have been so confused in his grief that
he bumped into Coloradolians on the
streets,

But,

and here's the point,

he would
have had a few more pleasant moments,
Because of the delicious flavor in Mrs.
Baker's pickles.

sacred to
THE MEMORY OF
THOMAS
ONETWO

xli

After Miss Brasblanc had rejected Thomas Onetwo, he decided no honest man would try to become President of the United States today, that he could never find THE source of all the sorrows of the American people, and that his perfect lady no longer existed, so he shot himself.

Now,

      if that man Thomas Onetwo had eaten a jar of Mrs. Baker's pickles, he undoubtedly would have seen no reason for committing suicide,

      Because of the delicious flavor in Mrs. Baker's pickles.